BUB AND CHUB

All inquiries should be addressed to:
Barron's Educational Series, Inc.
250 Wireless Boulevard
Hauppauge, NY 11788

International Standard Book Number 0-8120-4859-8

Library of Congress Catalog Card Number 91-41678

Library of Congress Cataloging-in-Publication Data

Foster, Kelli C.
  Bub and Chub/ by Foster & Erickson; illustrations by Kerri Gifford.
    p. cm. (Get ready—get set—read!)
    Summary: Invites the reader to guess where bear and lion cubs
Bub and Chub are while they are making hubbub as they scrub
and go "Glub."
  ISBN 0-8120-4859-8
    (1. Bears—Fiction.   2. Lions—Fiction.   3. Baths—Fiction.
4. Literary recreations.   5. Stories in rhyme.) I. Erickson, Gina Clegg.
II. Russell, Kerri Gifford, ill. III. Title. IV. Series: Erickson, Gina Clegg.
Get ready—get set—read!
PZ8.3.F813Bu 1992
(E)—dc20   91-41678
                                                                      CIP
                                                                      AC

PRINTED IN HONG KONG
5 9927 9876

GET READY...GET SET...READ!

BUB AND CHUB

by
Foster & Erickson

Illustrations by
Kerri Gifford

FOREST HOUSE™
School & Library Edition

This is Bub.

This is Chub.
They are both cubs.

But *where* are they?

Are Bub and Chub in space?

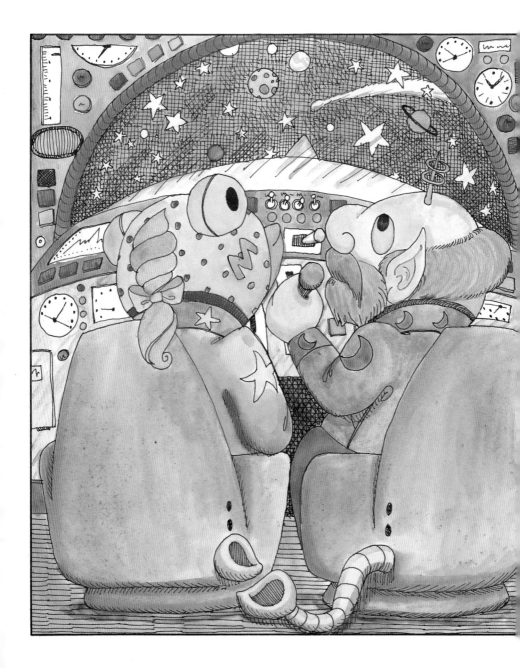

No cubs!
The cubs are not here.

Are the cubs in the woods?

No cubs!
Here is a hint: hubbub.

Are they making a hubbub
in the club?

No cubs!
Here is a hint: glub-glub.

Glub-glub.
Are the cubs in a sub?

No cubs!
Here is a hint: scrub.

Do the cubs scrub by
the shrubs?

No cubs!
Here is a hint: tub.

Are Bub and Chub
in the tub?

Yes! Rub-a-dub-dub,
two cubs in a tub.

The End

The UB Word Family

Bub
Chub
club
cubs
glub-glub
hubbub
rub-a-dub-dub
scrub
shrubs
sub

Sight Words

by
is
are
both
hint
they
this
space
woods
making

Dear Parents and Educators:

Welcome to *Get Ready...Get Set...Read!*

We've created these books to introduce children to the magic of reading.

Each story in the series is built around one or two word families. For example, *A Mop for Pop* uses the OP word family. Letters and letter blends are added to OP to form words such as TOP, LOP, and STOP. As you can see, once children are able to read OP, it is a simple task for them to read the entire word family. In addition to word families, we have used a limited number of "sight words." These are words found to occur with high frequency in the books your child will soon be reading. Being able to identify sight words greatly increases reading skill.

You might find the steps outlined on the facing page useful in guiding your work with your beginning reader.

We had great fun creating these books, and great pleasure sharing them with our children. We hope *Get Ready...Get Set...Read!* helps make this first step in reading fun for you and your new reader.

Kelli C. Foster, PhD
Educational Psychologist

Gina Clegg Erickson, MA
Reading Specialist

Guidelines for Using *Get Ready...Get Set...Read!*

Step 1.   Read the story to your child.

Step 2.   Have your child read the Word Family list aloud several times.

Step 3.   Invent new words for the list. Print each new combination for your child to read. Remember, nonsense words can be used (*dat, kat, gat*).

Step 4.   Read the story *with* your child. He or she reads all of the Word Family words; you read the rest.

Step 5.   Have your child read the Sight Word list aloud several times.

Step 6.   Read the story *with* your child again. This time he or she reads the words from both lists; you read the rest.

Step 7.   Your child reads the entire book to you!

Titles in the

Series:

SET 1

Find Nat
The Sled Surprise
Sometimes I Wish
A Mop for Pop
The Bug Club
BRING-IT-ALL-TOGETHER BOOKS
What a Day for Flying!
Bat's Surprise

SET 2

The Tan Can
The Best Pets Yet
Pip and Kip
Frog Knows Best
Bub and Chub
BRING-IT-ALL-TOGETHER BOOKS
Where Is the Treasure?
What a Trip!

SET 3

Jake and the Snake
Jeepers Creepers
Two Fine Swine
What Rose Does Not Know
Pink and Blue
BRING-IT-ALL-TOGETHER BOOKS
The Pancake Day
Hide and Seek

SET 4

Whiptail of Blackshale Trail
Colleen and the Bean
Dwight and the Trilobite
The Old Man at the Moat
By the Light of the Moon
BRING-IT-ALL-TOGETHER BOOKS
Night Light*
The Crossing*

SET 5

Tall and Small
Bounder's Sound*
How to Catch a Butterfly*
Ludlow Grows Up*
Matthew's Brew
BRING-IT-ALL-TOGETHER BOOKS
Snow in July*
Let's Play Ball*

* Forthcoming title